To Tiff

The Prison Plumb Line

Yvonne J. Medley

Bless you, and
The work you do ! :)

Yvonne J. Medley

Yvonne J. Medley © 2005, *Lessons Learned*

Copyright © 2011 Yvonne J. Medley
All rights reserved.

ISBN: 1-4637-6639-4
ISBN-13: 9781463766399

Dedication

This story is dedicated to *Angels Unawares*, incarcerated or not. Each one, lift one!

And the Lord said unto me, Amos what seest thou? And I said, "A plumbline." Then said the Lord, "Behold, I will set a plumbline in the midst of my people Israel: I will not again pass by them any more." Amos 7:8 KJV

Acknowledgements

To my earthly Lord and Savior, my husband, Robert Medley Sr., thank you for not only cheering me on, but also for your constant love, understanding and care of me, and our children. I believe that's called unconditional love, and a rich blessing.

I will forever appreciate my family and friends who truly lived for me, "…faith is the substance of things hoped for and the evidence of things not seen." (Hebrews 11:1). Even when I treaded frustration, doubt and giving up, you carried me until I felt strong enough to keep it moving. Thank you to my sister, Yvette Cetasaan and brother-in-law, Kwaku and Jordin; sister-in-law, Cheryl Medley-McKinney; Tom Saunders, Billy Medley, Leon and Patricia Dorsey, Nathaniel Williams, Love and Angela Smith, Cynthia Mazyck, Renée Dames, Chaplain John Lewis, Bishop and Mrs. Forrest Stith, Peggy Evans, and Cornell and Gloria Evans. Thanks to my parents Juanita Freeman and the Late Will S. Freeman for making certain, I focus on joy, not pain.

Thank you to the editor who got everything off the ground, Karen Sorenson-Bartelt and for constantly reminding me, "You said that already!" She taught me to trust my writing.

To my international encouragers, Katerina Llioglou in Australia, Michelle Higdon in London, Tokunbo Oladeinde, simply a Nigerian Yoruba Queen, and Maysa Elshafei, an Egyptian beauty, inside and out, a heartfelt thank you.

Thank you to my literary coaches/angels of the Life Journeys Writers Club; Emily Ferren, director of the Charles County Public Library (and her crew); the Lifelong Learning Center, The Enoch Pratt Free Library (Baltimore), author Ann Crispin and her husband, Michael. You not only encouraged and critiqued, but also imparted wisdom.

To the shepherds who ushered me in His presence, thank you to the Late Rev. Mannie L. Wilson, Convent Avenue Baptist Church (Harlem, N.Y.) and the Rev. Dr. and Mrs. William C. Calhoun, Sr., Trinity Baptist Church (Baltimore)—and to the shepherds who keep me in His presence, Pastor and Mrs. Darin V. Poullard, Fort Washington Baptist Church (*FWBC*) (Fort Washington, Md.). Thank you for sturdy lessons in integrity, love and patience as well as grace and mercy. Also thank you for your willingness to address the tough questions. To the *FWBC* Deacons and, especially the *FWBC* Women's Ministry, I'm grateful for your covering, objectivity and support.

###

Preface

FIVE WOMEN: MODUS OPERANDI (M.O.)—*Angels, Unawares*

Evie Freeman, 21
RACE: Black **EYES/HAIR** brown/black **HT/WT:** 5' 5"/111 lbs
    Starved for love and validation, Evie Freeman makes a habit of selling herself short. Freeman is beautiful and blessed with distinctive features, but doesn't know it. She's uncomfortable in her walnut skin, so there's been no shortage of man-trouble, toxic friendships and family drama. If she has any talents, natural or otherwise, she doesn't think much of them. Because—after all—if *she* can do them, can't everybody? Her drug-dealing lover lands her in jail.
External Encouragement: negative.
Confidence level: zero.
Confusion: rampant.
Future prospects: none.

Cookie Mendoza, 30
RACE: Hispanic **EYES/HAIR** green/brown **HT/WT** 5' 6"/145 lbs
    Cookie Mendoza worked her way up from bank teller to chief financial officer of special accounts at the Federal Credit Union, Headquarters/Washington, D.C. Mendoza is extremely competent and driven. She earned the respect

of her colleagues and forced the recognition of executives, not accustomed to regarding Latinos as their equal.

In her private life, Mendoza is severely quartered by a difficult divorce, a rebellious teenager, a dying mother, and the guardianship of her 17-year-old crack-addicted sister. The pressure to portray professional perfection rivals the pressure to keep private imperfections undetected. Expenses mount and threaten exposure. A solution arises; Embezzlement. Mendoza is exposed, attempting to restore the pilfered accounts. The federal offense is punishable by no less than fifteen years in prison.

External Encouragement: negative.
Confidence level: zero.
Confusion: through-the-roof.
Future Prospects: none.

Anne Sulley, 21
RACE: White **EYES/HAIR** green/black **HT/WT** 5' 7"/120 lbs.

Anne Sulley was adopted as an infant by a young, childless couple. A year after the adoption, her new mother unexpectedly conceived and gave birth to twin daughters. Later she bore a son. Sulley grew up feeling slightly out of place in the family. Her physical attributes, a slender, shapely and refined body, embodied in creamy orchid skin, stood out. Her natural talents in art and math were downplayed to keep her siblings secure.

On Christmas day, during a family gathering an intoxicated aunt blurted out the details of Sulley's adoption. Sulley, 16, was the only one who didn't know. Rebellion ensued; bad crowds, self-hatred, substance abuse, petty crimes shaped her world. At 18, Sulley left home for good, much to the relief of her parents. At 19, she married a man who abused her whenever the drunken impulse hit him. At 21 and divorced, and desperate for shelter, Sulley propositions an undercover cop, who arrests her. He takes seven stitches in the forehead from Sulley's stiletto heel. She receives an 18-month jail sentence.

External Encouragement: negative.
Confidence Level: zero.
Confusion: through-the-roof.
Future prospects: none.

Delta Dover, 20
RACE: Black **EYES/HAIR** brown/black **HT/WT** 5′ 6″/150 lbs.

Delta Dover was reared in a God-fearing, upper middle-class home and showered with all the love, support and possessions her parents could afford. But that wasn't enough. Dover is a know-it-all brat, who can't stand correction, especially from her parents. However, she possesses an angelic Hershey chocolate face, a sultry voice and a charismatic personality among her peers. She's the most popular in school. Dover excels, educationally, right to premed.

She is on her way to becoming a doctor, when a detour sends her to jail. In an airport, during the Thanksgiving semester break, Dover's trip is diverted by two sniffing K-9s. They take a liking to the package sewn into the lining of her jacket. Sentencing arrives on Dover's twentieth birthday. Amid a backdrop of sniffling parents, and praying church members the Judge renders his qualitative two cents. "I know you're in for a life change," he says, "whether it's good or bad, that's up to you." Dover rolls her eyes at him and mumbles under her breath, "Thanks. You've ruined my life. Now shut up."

External Encouragement: positive.
Confidence level: false.
Confusion: through-the-roof.
Future prospects: none.

Rosalie Mandy, 25
RACE: Biracial **EYES/HAIR** brown/black **HT/WT** 5′ 6″/135 lbs.

Rosalie Mandy's birth was the product of her white mother's rape by a black man. Her mother decides to keep her third child, but can barely stand to look at her. Mandy's eyes have the look of a cruel stranger's. Her huge marble eyes, olive skin and curly, jet-black hair paint a beautiful portrait to the unknowing, but to her fair-haired family they bear indictment. Her "dad" tries to overlook his fleshy reminder of the night he laid bound and gagged, unable to protect his wife, but he can't. He divorces the family when Mandy is five. The tiny community she lives in never shuns her, just pities her like an abandoned puppy. Mandy grows up love-starved and lacking self-worth. At 21, Mandy flees her hometown for better prospects, but finds none. Instead, she's USDA prime for every user/loser, male and female, that dances her way.

Coming from a party, about 3 .a.m., Mandy's two newfound girlfriends decide that she is too drunk/high to drive her car. Jesa, minus a valid driver's license, hijacks the wheel. On a dark, two-lane backstreet, while Mandy lay passed out in the backseat, Jesa hits a young man on a bicycle. The man is on his way to work at Seven-Eleven. Jesa powers the accelerator, leaving the injured man alone and dying. The next morning, the police knock on Mandy's apartment door, handcuffs her and she's off to jail. Jesa disappears.

External Encouragement: negative.
Confidence level: zero.
Confusion: through-the-roof.
Future prospects: none.

chapter

ONE

Evie Freeman had three or four aliases and several outstanding warrants in Maryland, Virginia and the District of Columbia by the time the cops caught her climbing out of a bathroom window at The Plainview Motel. Evie and her boyfriend, Ray, were in room twenty-eight, lounging on its faded plaid couch, bored and staring at a rerun of *Good Times* on television. Outside, just a few doors away, three police cars rolled up the gravel driveway, sirenless, and stopped short at the manager's office. Six police officers spilled out. Three officers bum rushed the pasty-faced manager, who flushed maroon at the sight of them. Moments prior, he too had been bored, sitting lifeless and staring at a rerun of *Gilligan's Island* on his tiny television screen. One of the officers was polite, but stern when he outstretched a piece of threefold paper touching the manager's chest. "We have a warrant to search the premises," the police officer said.

The maroon drained white as the startled old man, now standing, extended a trembling hand to receive the piece of paper. He responded, "Huh?" But he heard what the officer said.

"Do you have a Ray Johnson or a Evie Freeman registered here?" the officer asked, studying the old man's facial expressions for the truth. Wisely, the old man stood there adopting the expression of looking like he had to search his memory. Search warrants were regular occurrences at The Plainview. First and foremost on his mind was the skillful art of non-self-incrimination. So he needed precious time to think.

The manager's private thought was *hell no, I don't know'em*. What he said was, "Well now, officer, lemme think." Based on the police officer's descriptions, the manager's memory refreshed and he told the officers where they could find Evie and Ray. Before the old man could complete his last sentence, the officers turned, one said something on a walkie talkie, and they beelined for room twenty-eight.

When the fierce banging erupted on the door of Ray and Evie's motel room, the violent noise rifled through their intestines and ignited gut reactions from the both of them. They knew what to do. Amid a serenade of toilet water flushing, the front door burst open just as Ray was shoving Evie out of the bathroom window. She was cascading sideways and noticed the sudden absence of Ray's assistance, but she kept the flow. It was a muggy, melting August night. Even the flies were down to a slow crawl. Only the delicate privates of Evie's petite body were thinly veiled in cut-off jeans and a halter top. Without warning, she literally fell into the waiting arms of a police officer, dropping like a ripe apple falling from a tree. She smelled of baby powder, the officer noticed. It tickled his nose. He worked to dismiss it, while pulling out his handcuffs.

The two were hiding out just outside of town because their house had been raided about two months earlier. The Plainview seemed like the perfect spot. It was an economic stain, blotted upon Maryland's scenic southbound route of 301. It was so distasteful, the U-shaped dilapidated building stood invisible to most travelers. The motel boasted *Clean Sheets!! Hourly Rates!!* on a lit-up portable marquee, positioned in a grassy ditch.

On the Sunday evening Evie and Ray were arrested, the police had raided their house for a third time. Evie and Ray weren't there, of course, but some of Ray's friends, employees and loyal clientele were. Everyone was just sitting around, chilling and watching the game on the flat screen. A continuous flow of music from the CD player peppered the air as they swigged beer, got high and philosophied over nothing. Even when he wasn't around, Ray was a good host and businessman. He always kept plenty of social get-high around to keep folks sampling and buying, and the frig was always stocked with plenty of beer. Ray practiced an open-door policy. Evie's younger sister, Roni, was there, making herself at home, too. She was cornrowing her five-year-old daughter's hair. Her two-year-old son played with toy trucks at her feet.

Suddenly, a big hard knock irrupted on the door and exploded it off its hinges. "Charles County Sheriff," shouted one of several police officers bunched up on the front porch. Guns were drawn. The aftershock of the door banging shook the pictures off the wall, halted the music and killed the mellow vibe all-up-in-there. In an instant, folks shook off their buzz and scrambled. They knew what to do. They were well rehearsed like well-rehearsed ballerinas showing off in a Nutcracker recital. Toilets flushed, upstairs and down, as fast as the blue water could stop, drop and swirl. White powder misted the air on the way down, while prime-grade weed simply drowned and twirled its way out of sight. Freshly snuffed-out blunts got hidden beneath under-folds of tender breasts inside bra cups or shoved down underpants and planted between warm butt cheeks that got a lot warmer. Roni shoved the blunt she was enjoying in her huge jar of dark brown hair gel. It was sitting on the table beside her and she was using it to firm up her daughter's braids. The blunt sizzled like a French fry, dropped in a pan of hot grease. Roni slammed the jar's lid down and twisted it shut.

Mrs. Wiggins, next door, watched the drama unfold by peeking through her kitchen window. Her ample frame was now girdle-free and comfortable, after having consumed a full serving of good preaching down at her church. Her body jiggled when she ran to the window at the first sound of commotion. She caught the third and final unmarked car power to an abrupt halt on Ray's front lawn. Mrs. Wiggins was clad in her famous sky blue housedress with the polka dots and hadn't yet taken off her big brown fluffy wig. She looked like the momma bear of the Berenstain Bears.

Mrs. Wiggins, it was widely known, kept an eye on everything that went on in the neighborhood. When she noticed the three midnight blue unmarked cars, she cracked open her kitchen window just a sliver and ordered her three grandkids inside the house. It took only minutes for her to rush to the front door, open it, swallow them inside and rush back to her viewing spot. She ordered the children upstairs to her back bedroom/sewing room in case of gunfire. They knew the drill. She borrowed an extra moment to turn down the fire under her collard greens and frying pork chops. Then she nestled in her ringside seat to watch the action. Mrs. Wiggins earned her master's in snoopology years ago. She knew how to crease her yellow curtains just enough to acquire the perfect viewpoint of almost anything she needed to see, yet remain undetected. Keeping watch over the neighborhood was her official, unassigned civic duty.

As far as the neighborhood was concerned, Ray's house was a danger zone, a crack-house cordoned off with invisible tape. Strangers marched in and out of there during all hours of the day and night. Loud noises and music often escaped its walls and cars burned rubber from its curbside without warning. It was a menace to the entire community. Everybody wanted it gone. But it felt just as dangerous to do something about it as it did to live with it. Dropping a dime on Ray's crack-house could get a gal hurt. Becoming a witness to anything that went on in there could get a fellow dead. One afternoon, Ray caught a neighbor, Old Mr. Harley glued to the sidewalk, scouring into his personal business deal. Ray looked down from his porch and said, directly, "snitches get stitches, old man," Mr. Harley suddenly became unglued and stepped lively. And so, all the God-fearing people in the neighborhood decided to let God handle it—while they stayed clear.

During the drug raid, the police didn't really get much in the way of confiscated evidence. They missed out on some good hard stuff, too, stashed away in zip lock baggies, buried in six large peanut butter jars. The jars were placed here-and-there in the kitchen cupboards amongst general groceries. Apparently, the police didn't wonder why the place was so well stocked with peanut butter. At least one box of elbow macaroni contained a small handgun. But the police weren't really looking for *stuff* to bag, anyway. They knew there were drugs in the place. The police weren't looking to net mindless druggies either. They were looking for prime, grade 'A' flesh. They wanted to decapitate the head of the operation, the crack house menacing their turf. They wanted Ray.

At least two other little boys, along with Roni's son and daughter, were inside the house that day. It broke Mrs. Wiggins's heart to see them panicked and crying. They were huddled around a policewoman's leg as she held them at bay, while plain-clothes cops rushed all the adults out onto the front lawn. One by one, Ray's houseguests were ordered to lie face down and spread-eagle on the grass. Three women and five men were frisked and handcuffed. They were handled off the ground and stuffed into the extra patrol cars that had zoomed up. It was a well-choreographed ballet. While all that was going on, two of the police officers went back inside the house to give it one more search. They didn't seem to carry out anything, but, according to Mrs. Wiggins's report, later, to the head of the homeowners' association, "They must have found something because suddenly they whisked outta there like bats out of hell." Mrs. Wiggins was nearly breathless from the excitement of relaying the tale. "They must have picked up on something juicy because they all rushed out of there in a hurry," she said this time with arm movements to accent the retelling of the account. It was not lost on Mrs. Wiggins, either, that Ray and Evie were not amongst the group arrested. The whole scene was about an hour's worth of noisy spectacle, she estimated.

There wasn't a visible eye in sight that day, but just about everyone in the neighborhood watched with gleeful amazement. Descriptive accounts mushroomed and graced their dining room tables for weeks. "Yeah, they arrested about thirty druggies over there," one woman recounted during choir rehearsal. Most neighbors, though, also understood that since the police hadn't apprehended Ray and Evie, the spectacle mainly served as a calling card for the infamous couple.

What the police did find was a Plainview matchbook stuck between the couch cushions at Ray's house. That's what sent them racing southbound on Route 301.

About three hours after the raid, just as dusk moved over the neighborhood's rooftops, Jamar, a little guy who lived up the street appeared out of nowhere. Jamar attends the same high school as Mrs. Wiggins's fifteen-year-old granddaughter, Cammie. He walked up to the giant silver street lamp, standing on a patch of curb grass right in front of Mrs. Wiggins's front porch. He gazed upon it for a second, caressed it with his arms and legs, and inched his long skinny body upward, like a slinky, until he reached the top. With one arm and both legs curled tightly around the pole, Jamar ripped off a package that was taped to the side of the light bulb's silver casing. He tucked it under his chin and slithered quickly back down the pole with little effort. Mrs. Wiggins was standing out on her porch, getting some air when all this happened. She was skillfully maneuvering a toothpick between her two back teeth, trying to extract a bit of melted macaroni and cheese. She was also studying Jamar. Just before he mounted the lamppost, he turned and gave her a chilling stare. Now, Mrs. Wiggins could remember when she used to babysit him and diaper that boy's bottom, but just the same, she heeded his warning and sauntered back inside the house. She resumed her inspection through her carefully creased kitchen curtains.

Jamar was fetching Ray's main crude drug inventory, and a list of important names, numbers, accounts and lawyers. It was a task Jamar had been pre-instructed and pre-paid quite well to do in case of an emergency. The police raid constituted an emergency. Part two of his mission was to find a new hiding place for the package, keep his mouth shut and wait for further instructions.

chapter

TWO

Back at The Plainview Motel, post police raid, with a policeman at each arm, Evie was escorted to a waiting patrol car. Its blaring amber and blue overhead lights circled the perimeter of the motel and competed with the glow of its marquee sign. It also summoned a scruffy crowd of curious onlookers. One policeman palmed Evie's head and lowered it as she folded her body into his patrol car. Quickly, she searched for and spied a deflated-looking Ray already nestled in the fenced-in backseat of a second patrol car. Their eyes met for only seconds, but his message to Evie was clear; *don't talk*. The ride to county jail was swift and uneventful. And it was a good thing, too, because the big silver bolt of the handcuffs had rested against the small of Evie's back and it hurt. She also had to pee. At the jail, she expected to see Ray, but didn't. Not finding him, felt like a punch in the gut.

The booking process is a humiliating, out-of-body experience by most accounts. However, the humiliation only kicks in for those who feel above it. First, there is disbelief. Then prayers go out for expediency. "Lord, please, please…please Lord, get me outta here," Evie heard someone chanting while being escorted through the jail's lobby. And third, prays for anonymity flourish. Sadly, fate grants little, if anything at all. There's a cavity search, complete with a buck-naked squat-n-cough. Wrap that up in a bright orange jumpsuit (one size fits most), and the humiliation is clear. The experience, Evie noted, is also laced with hours of unexplained waiting time while cuffed to a big silver chain bolted to the wall. But, again, if the arrested party is used to handing over life and loins to just any circumstance, then the booking process is just an annoying formality.

During the booking process Evie was brain-dead. She fumbled through the formalities like a zombie. She sat and/or stood motionless unless someone came to fetch her one way or the other. After about three hours, she finally gave up hope of seeing Ray. Her spirit refreshed when she caught a brief glimpse of her younger sister. Roni was sitting across the hall in a tiny holding room identical to the one Evie was in. Like Evie, she sat on a bench, handcuffed to a thick silver chain protruding out of the wall. Roni, only nineteen, was crying and working hard to wipe her eyes on the sleeve of her orange jumpsuit. At the sight of Roni, Evie allowed her own eyes to well up. She tried to get Roni's attention without alerting the surrounding officers, but she was unsuccessful. A policewoman came into view and led Roni out of sight like a puppy on a leash. Seeing her sister was all Evie needed to put two and two together, and realize that Ray's house had been raided. *That's how the police caught up with us*, she thought to herself. Ugly visions swarmed in her head. "How could I have done this to Roni," she whispered to herself as her tears fell and spotted the front of her jumpsuit with tiny burnt-orange circles. Evie found out, about a week later, through her lawyer, that Roni had only spent that evening in custody, as did everyone else who was apprehended at the house that Sunday. But Roni did not regain custody of her children. Social Services had stepped in. It kept tabs on her whereabouts and forced her to find a new job because stripping in the town's only nudie bar was not considered desirable employment. Roni also had to take classes in parenting skills, if she wanted her children back. There was one other condition too, unbeknownst to Evie.

"Roni," said the social worker assigned to the case, "you must agree not to have any contact with your older sister, Evie, for at least twenty-four months." Roni stared at the woman, openmouthed. "Understood?" The social worker said sternly.

A meek and mild Roni repeated, "Understood." Her gaze dropped to the floor.

While being escorted to Cellblock K, Evie was only conscious of the rhythmic scraping noise her plastic jail-issue sandals made against the granite floor. Her cell was a 6 x 10 rectangle and painted a dull piss yellow. A cot was positioned on opposite walls with a bare thin, dingy mattress atop its springs. Evie carried a crisp set of linens and a blanket for the cot she would use.

"You're in luck, Freeman," said the female corrections officer—C.O.s, they called them. Evie took notice that the formality of "Miss" which satirized every greeting during her booking was abandoned in the lock-up. She wouldn't hear it garnish her name again.

"Looks like you got a single suite!" The C.O. coughed up a cold dry, laugh to salt her next comment, "But don't count on that for long, honey. Hurry up and make your bed. It's Light's Out in thirty minutes. Morning comes in early around here," she added, as she slammed the door shut and walked away. The jingle of her keys echoed down the hall.

Among other things, Evie went to bed hungry that night. They gave her a bag lunch, earlier, in the holding cell. The tuna looked and smelled like vomit packed between two pieces of hard bread. Evie ate it, but she failed to keep it down. Thank God for the toilet, she thought, right next to the bench where she sat handcuffed.

Day 30—one month in. Evie finally found herself standing before a judge. Prior to her day in court, she'd only had three visits from the outside. She saw her public defender lawyer once, her mother twice. The lawyer, a skinny, nervous looking white man, who looked eleven, came to prep her for her court appearance. She could not have cared less. He also told her that Ray was in a lot of trouble. She perked up a bit to hear news about Ray. Lawyer and client sat across from each other in a small room that resembled a closet. The table between them took up most of the space.

"Your boyfriend is being charged with murder," the lawyer said, "The police were able to link an overdose death to the drugs he sold." He talked slow so he could study Evie's face for a telling expression. There was none. He continued, "Yeah, it seems that crack he sold was loaded with PCP." He paused, waiting for Evie to react with shock or give a look that said she knew he often toyed with his customers, but she didn't flinch to that either. He continued, "... Well, it killed some poor guy who used it."

Evie broke eye contact and stared at the table. Frustrated, the lawyer started acting fidgety, like he had somewhere else to be. He dropped the glibness, peeked at his watch and moved in closer to her face. "Evie," he said, "look at me. The judge wants your boyfriend's supplier even more than he wants your boyfriend. And he doesn't really want *you* at all. If you tell what you know, Evie, you could get a reduced sentence or maybe even get out of here all together. Whadda ya say?" Evie said nothing. About five seconds marched by and the lawyer got the message. He pushed his chair out, checked his watch again and stood up to repack his briefcase. The little Opie Taylor lookalike pushed the intercom button to let the C.O. know that he was finished, fed up and ready to get out. He glared at Evie who really wasn't looking up at his face and said, "Then don't count on seeing your boyfriend or your freedom for a while."

Evie's eyes followed his movements, then wadded with moisture before tears fell down her blank face.

The eleven-looking-year-old stopped and said to her softly, "Look, I know you're a good kid and I know you're afraid. Your boyfriend is toast—whether you say something or not. So he can't hurt you, Evie. But you're gonna have to help me help you." There was silence. Her tears kept falling, but she never parted her lips. Then he sighed and said, "I'll see what I can do." He gave her an awkward smile, signaled the waiting C.O. to unlock the door. He left.

Evie's mother came to visit twice. Her mother couldn't stand Ray and the two of them, mother and daughter, had several physical blowups about it. Just before Evie's arrest the two weren't speaking to each other. That first visit at the jail was strained at best. Her mother blinked back tears at the sight of her daughter in jail. She practically bit her tongue, trying not to say, "I told you so." When her mother finally mustered up some conversation, she said, "God will get you through this." But neither of them believed that nonsense.

Evie offered a weak smile and thought, *Yeah? How? How will He get me through this?* She kept silent because it seemed like a moot point. She was glad to see her mother, in a funny sort of way. She didn't know why, since her mother mostly acted like her children were inconveniences.

Evie sat before her mother in uneasy silence. She was unable to shake the memory of their last argument. It was a screaming match of accusations, obscenities and blows. Evie kept defending her relationship with Ray, while her mother sentenced Ray to hell and promised to put him there. The finale came when her mother shouted, "Why don't you get the hell out of my house and call me when you wake up out of your damn fog." That's when Evie moved in with Ray—wholly.

Their second jail visit didn't go much better. Lying in her cell reminiscing about it, Evie thought, *Well Ma, I'm out of my fog now. But what's the point?*

chapter

THREE

"Eighteen months, plus restitution on one-half of $6,660," Judge Butler declared from the bench. He gave a little sermon, as well. "Miss Freeman, you need this jail time," he said, "to clear your head." Evidently, he thought she was in a fog, too. "And if you need a little more time," Judge Butler preached, "just let me know. A smart young lady like you, only twenty-one years old, shouldn't have such rogues for friends—or should you be running around with a drug-pushing boyfriend. You could have a bright future and an honest life if that's what you wanted." She stood before him, blank.

The sentence the Judge gave her was also meant to jolt her into turning state's evidence against Ray. Even from the bench, Judge Butler hinted that Evie could get probation and/or a lighter sentence if she cooperated with the court, but she didn't go for it. So the judge sent her away for possession of stolen goods and check fraud.

On the day, she and Ray were arrested their motel room was loaded with electronics, gadgets and stuff. One of the arresting police officers joked, "They must have been trying to put Circuit City out of business!" Televisions, DVD players, DVDs, CDs, appliances, cell phones, and more, gathered dust in every nook-n-cranny of the tiny room. They either stole, outright, or purchased everything using stolen credit cards and checks. Some of it was hot merchandise that Ray's customers often used as currency when cash was tight. The merchandise turned out to be a pretty good sideline for Ray. He was ever the entrepreneur.

As Evie was led away, she quickly scanned the courtroom for sightings of Ray, or Roni, or her mother, but she saw no one. It was her final confirmation that she was on her own and on her way to hell.

Day 50—almost two months in. Evie had settled into the jail routine pretty well. It took her every bit of those first thirty-some-odd days to learn how to conquer her food, gagless, and keep it down. She also had to get used to eating breakfast at 5:30 a.m., lunch at 11 a.m. and dinner at 4:30 p.m. *These fools are ridiculous*, she thought, *who gets up at 5:30 in the butt-crack of dawn.*

If she could stay on good behavior, she was told, she would eventually get work release. That meant working and eating at a nearby fast food restaurant or factory, and earning about $5 an hour.

The highlight for the inmates came when commissary time rolled around. Family members deposited limited amounts of money into accounts for the women and they could buy snacks, notebooks, stationary and stamps. Mail was generally issued during that time, as well. But Evie never got any mail and no one ever put anything into her account. Evie was eventually assigned to work in the jail's laundry. She earned a day off her sentence for each month she worked and exhibited good behavior. She also earned 80 cents an hour, but most of that went toward her court fees, restitution and her rent at the jail. It shocked her to learn that she had to pay room-and-board for her cell. She did have some money to buy candy and stuff, but rarely did. She just wasn't in the mood for frivolous fancies.

There was the rec room for exercising and a dayroom for congregating. It shared a television perched high on a steel shelf, firmly chained and bolted, and minus its knobs. Both rooms offered dreary existences. Thank God, Evie noted, that she had freewill to choose whether she wanted to be in either—most of the time. But she had to eat her meals in the dayroom and it took her a while to figure out how not to get her behind kicked for breakfast, lunch and dinner. Apparently, the other women mistook her self-imposed isolation for a snubbing and they didn't care for it. First, would come a good cussing out, which she got on the regular. Second, came a threat of violence. The C.O.s always managed to come to her rescue just before the threats spiraled into action. Third, Evie would finish her meal under the watchful eye of the C.O., then retreat back to her cell.

That was the routine. On the positive, the Charles County Correctional Facility offered GED classes. Evie quit high school after she took up with Ray. She met him when she was only seventeen. After her sentencing, she decided to sign up for the GED classes. She was bored and it gave her something to do. Evie liked to read, she remembered that, so she took advantage of the visits to the jail's library, too. The jail also offered anger-management classes and classes on life-skills, but she didn't want to overload herself.

Evie used every bit of those fifty days or so to practice being alone. After all, this was how she planned to spend the rest of her life, whether incarcerated or not. She ate alone, exercised alone, sat in the dayroom alone, and cried alone in her cell. And it wasn't because she thought she was, "too f'n' good to talk to anybody," as one fellow inmate suggested. It was because she was just too "f'n'" hopeless and heartbroken to strike up normal conversation with anyone, like everything was all right. To her credit, Evie was spending her alone time trying to figure out how she'd gotten into such a mess. Jail, she discovered, possessed a rear-view mirror quality to it.

After sentencing, Evie returned to jail, one dimensional. She barely even felt like a human being. She walked up to her cell, led only by the C.O.'s prompts. He had to lift her hands so he could remove the handcuffs. When he did, her hands dropped to her side, lifeless. Evie flopped down onto the cot, belly first, like a discarded rag doll. That day she passed up lunch and laid there, crosswise, staring downward at the granite tile floor. Protruding between her mattress and the aluminum coils, at its edge, was of a beat-up old book. Evie spied it, curiously. "How'd that get there," she spoke softly to herself, shifting her weight just a little to pry the book loose. *Holy Bible* was printed in bold black letters across its worn-out front cover. Evie rolled over with book in hand and inspected it for a moment or two. She wondered how it got there. She wondered how long had it been there and why she hadn't noticed or felt it beneath her before. Slowly she opened it and turned to its first two pages. She found them littered with autographed scribblings and outlined patches of scriptures and verse. Evie quickly fanned through its pages to find more of the same drenched in rainbow highlights of yellow, pink, and blue. There were also tiny drawings. Hearts, stick figures, happy faces, even tear drops appeared throughout its pages. She fingered them with amazement. The first note she read was scribbled, very tiny, in the top right-hand margin of the Bible's inside flap. It was signed by someone named Delta Dover.

Evie spent that night scouring the front pages of the Bible. She read the little snippets she found legible and then she turned to their scriptural references.

> *Only God and I control my destiny, no one else and we've decided to take it back! Delta Dover*

> *I'm sorry, God, for my sins. I ask for your forgiveness. Anne Sulley*

> *Thank you Jesus, for a second chance. I won't mess up this time. Cookie Mendoza. I've repented, like you said to do.*

I hate my father and my mother, too. But God I guess you know that. So please help me. I heard what you said in that scripture today (Roman's 19:12). So YOU handle the revenge. Right now, I want to kill them both. This is their fault. Rosalie Mandy

A couple of weeks went by and Evie had grown into a routine of inspecting the pages of her newfound Bible and pondering the notes. They were jotted down in tiny lettering, some in blue ink, some in red ink, some in colored pencil, some were even written in green ink. The notes were positioned in every direction imaginable, in every margin of almost every page. Each sentiment was authored. Some were boxed in.

RESIST THE DEVIL!! James 4:1 I'm resisting, Lord, but it's hard!!! Cookie

If you have the faith of Jesus, your prayers will be answered. Mat. 21:18-22/Mark11:12-14 & 20-26/ John 14:1-14/Psalm 145:19 Rosalie M.

Moses is dead! I will be there to help you, so step up to the plate. Joshua 1:2,5,9. Lord, I'm trying to forget the past, but how can I forget it when I'm stuck in here? Anne Sulley

Momma, I'm forgiving you. Can't you forgive me? Anne

Be Patient! Prov. 19:2-3 (What else can I do?) Cookie

That woman showed total brokenness. Matthew 15:21-28. Broken is what I am. Rosalie Mandy

Hebrews 10:19-39 GOT TO HOLD ON!! Delta Dover

Lying on her cot, she read the notes, over and over. She also poured over the scriptures they referenced. It was a good way to pass the time. She stared at the blank brick walls in her cell and wondered what these women looked like, what they must have done to get themselves locked up and what happened to them. *Maybe*, she thought, *they're still in here.* So for that reason, she kept her Bible discovery a secret, fearing a previous owner might see it and reclaim it. *These were some desperate, sad women,* Evie surmised, *to be scribbling in a Bible—like that was going to do them some good. And why'd they write their names in here? Stupid! How pathetic*, she thought. She kept on reading.

chapter

FOUR

Day 77—about two and a half months in. It was a Friday. Evie had polished off her solitary breakfast and retreated to her cell. This time it was without hostile interference. Things were looking up. The morning hours morphed into lunchtime. Like clockwork, the faint noise of food carts rattling outside the cellblock caused her to consider the possibilities of holding down a solitary lunch. Interrupting her thoughts was an announcement from the control desk.

"Bible Study Ladies. Tonight, in classroom three. If you're goin', come up here and put your name on the signup sheet. Now!" The muffled voice blared into the control desk microphone. It was Officer Stone, who made the announcement. *Stone's cool*, Evie thought, *at least she never talks down to us.* There were several C.O.s like that, Evie noticed. Stone did not usually make announcements on the loud speaker, so when Evie heard the familiar voice it aroused interest. As a rule, Evie ignored the announcements, except for the ones having to do with GED class or library visits.

I don't know why you jailbirds waste your time with that hocus pocus shit was Evie's usual thought whenever she heard announcements about Bible study or church. But on Day 77, without thinking, almost like she was a robot, Evie rolled herself into a sitting position on her cot and gave what she heard some thought. Evie slipped on her beige open-toed sandals.

Cellblock K configured a circle. The round opened space on the main floor constituted the dayroom area. A number of classrooms and the recreation room were embedded along the sides. The cells and the showers were on the upper two tiers and fully visible from the control desk on the main floor. During the day hours, the cell doors remained open. A luxury not afforded to some of the other cellblocks. Even though Evie's cell was close to the steps leading down to the main area, she walked full circle to get to the stairs, so she could think.

Once Evie made her decision, she walked down the steps and joined the line of women, waiting to write their names on the signup sheet. Her presence shocked the other women. Smart comments wanted to abound because there was no shortage of quick-wit circling, but shock sealed lips.

That evening, when the C.O. on duty came to round up the women for Bible study, Evie quietly joined the others, holding a crisp new, Chaplain-issued Bible folded in her arms. The women were frisked before and after the short walk to class. They leaned against the wall with their hands and feet spread-eagle.

Inside the classroom, the Church Lady greeted them with a broad smile, as if that was all it took to cure cancer, end wars, and pass out pardons. She would just *happy* their problems away. Evie took one look at the woman. *Oh yeah, that's right. I remember now*, she thought, *what a waste of time*. She let out a tiny sarcastic laugh to herself, which in itself was progress because she hadn't laughed at anything or barely spoke to anyone since she'd been in jail. She also changed her mind about being in the Bible Study, but knew that such indecision was not negotiable.

"How you ladies doing today?" the Church Lady cheerfully asked, as the women slowly sauntered in, some in orange jumpsuits, some in white and some in navy blue jumpsuits. The rhythmic sound of their sandals scraping against the granite floor preceded them.

"How you think I'm doing?" Evie answered, silently in her head, *"I'm in jail, you jackass!"* She slid her body into one of the classroom chairs, the kind with the desk attached. She sat in a seat apart from everyone else. It was her way of quietly making a statement. The Church Lady, probably in her late forties, understood Evie's protest move. She honed in on Evie's gesture as if it was a radar distress signal.

"What's goin' on girl? What's your name?"

"Evie," she responded with disdain in her voice.

Just because Evie had signed up to be there, didn't mean that she was sure about being in there and it certainly didn't mean that she had any intention to talk in front of these stupid, gullible losers. This woman had no right to assume otherwise. It was just curiosity, that's all, that pulled her in there. Evie screamed inside, *DON'T ask me anything else*.

The Church Lady ignored Evie's disdain. "Evie, huh. Well, what's up with you? How you dealing with all this? You look mad or something—pissed off at someone. Who you pissed at? You pissed off at God?" The Church Lady appeared to be suppressing a smirk, which infuriated Evie and tickled the other women in the room. They'd been through the drill before.

The room fell silent. All inmate eyes were on Evie and they were all chomping at the bit, waiting to see what was next. Evie tried staring the Church Lady down. Then she rolled her eyes. In between, she cut to her peripheral view to see if the other women were staring. They were. Not only could she feel their pupils burning holes in her jumpsuit, but also she could have sworn she saw a few of them salivate. To them getting a reaction out of Evie was a long overdue pleasure. The build-up was worth it. They ached to see it. The women dangled off the edge of their seats, waiting for the Church Lady to do what they couldn't—extract emotion out of a zombie.

Evie was taken aback by the questions. She was equally stunned that the Church Lady used the words *pissed* and *God* in the same sentence. *What kind of Church Lady was this, anyway? Where's her flowered dress and church hat with the fruit salad on top? Where's her huge Bible in the leather case; her weapon to stamp out all damnation and save souls?*

Why is she wearing jeans and sneakers? Why is her face painted in make-up? Why she got those big gold hoops in her ears, is that allowed? Does she think she's cute or something? Is that sacred, religious, huh? Questions popped up in her head like popcorn, *Is this woman for real?* That was her last question.

The Church Lady kept at her.

"Who ya pissed at, girl?" the Church Lady said, point-blank in her face, "Go on and say it. It's okay."

With that, Evie felt her eyes moisten. Her hands started to tremble, so she folded them up tightly in her lap. Her body heated. *Oh no, I can't cry in front of these losers*, she thought. Her innards went to war. Some of her organs wanted to collapse under the pressure. Some didn't. She tried to toughen up by rolling her eyeballs up in the air. Perhaps extra oxygen could dry them up. Seconds trudged by, but in slow motion. *Stop it! Stop it!* She screamed in her head. *SSShit!*

Then she composed herself—as best she could, so she could speak. "Look," Evie said with an attitude and a marble-eyed glare that said, *back-up off me*, "there ain't nothin' wrong with me. I ain't *dealing* with nothing. I just don't belong here, that's all." Faint snickers erupted behind her. "And if I *AM* pissed-off at God…," *That's right. I'm back in control now,* she thought. Evie was mad as hell, dishing out neck action while she talked. "…so what!" Evie said, "If there is a God, what good can He do me? I'm in here and that's that."

The drool was so plentiful around the room the slurping was nearly audible. Smirked expressions peppered the room and the collective undivided attention said it all. It screamed, "*OOOOOWEEEE, this is juicy!*"

The gauntlet had been thrown down: Church Lady, 1. Evie, 2, but the Church Lady refused to shrink back in defeat. Instead, she seemed aroused by the challenge. *DAMN IT*, Evie thought, she went in for the kill. "If He's supposed to be so good, like you people are always sayin'," Evie said, "then He shoulda kept me outta here. But He didn't, now did He. And can He—or you—tell me why I'm here? Why He let this happen to me?" *There*, Evie thought, letting go a satisfying sigh, *now get off my back. Maybe you'll shut-up and leave me the hell alone.* But Church Lady didn't.

Evie's belligerence intoxicated the Church Lady's spirit. She lived for debate like this. The other inmates snickered again because they already knew that. Instead of snuffing out the fire, Evie had fanned the flames. Usually when church folk got challenged they mostly got mad, declared you demonic and spouted off a bunch of spiritual gobbledygook. Then they fled the scene of the crime.

But who was this church-lady woman, slowly invading Evie's space, looking like she was really giving some thought to her outrage? The Church Lady told Evie that her anger was really a guise for fear. "And though you really don't expect answers to your questions," the Church Lady said, "you really need some answers. And here's some good news for ya, girl. You're gonna get them, too." The Church Lady paused for emphasis. "As soon as you're ready to hear them," she said. The room silence solidified.

"Well…," the Church Lady said, "what'd you say your name was? Huh? Evie? Oh Yeah, Evie. It's a good thing that you don't think you belong here because you don't, except for a couple of facts, and I'll tell you about those later."

WHAT? WHAT ARE THEY! TELL ME NOW! Evie's whole body screamed as she felt herself losing her cool again.

"But you *ARE* here, so what you gonna do about it?"

Oh yeah, right, Evie thought. *What was I thinking, here comes the gobbledygook. Woman, you ain't said nothin' yet.*

Evie was about to declare victory when the Church Lady continued on, "You need to get up off your pity pot, get tough and hold on, girl. The good news is that you don't have to do any of that by yourself. You can do all that using the God you're so pissed at. And, another thing, don't go blaming everything bad that happened to you on God... He didn't do it!"

Evie kept staring at her, not quite knowing what to think.

The Church Lady continued, "I know you think you're the walkin' dead."

HUH! Evie thought.

"But I don't see you lying in no coffin." The Church Lady let about a second lapse in silence, then fussed on, "And shoot, you blaming God, like you woulda listened to anything He had to tell you, anyway."

"You ain't my mother, woman. Who do you think you're talkin' to!" Evie said, louder than anyone had ever heard her speak. The other women gasped and giggled, and waited for the response to come. This was priceless— was the collective, spectator thought.

Undaunted, the Church Lady fired back, incredulously, "You mean to tell me ain't nobody ever tried to tell you something—before all this happened?" She hammered on, "Nobody told you that you needed to wake your behind up out of your fog and maybe drop some folks?" Now the Church Lady was using a little neck action and salted it with her signature attitude. Evie looked bewildered.

"But He *cannnn* get you out of all this mess if you want Him to and it doesn't really matter why you're here," the Church Lady's voice softened. "Evidently, Evie, this must be an important stop on your personal journey; one that God felt you needed to make so you could get your shhii…," she said.

HUH?? Oh no she didn't, Evie thought.

Right about now, shock was stamped across Evie's face to almost hear a curse word spew out of the mouth of someone teaching Bible Study. The other women giggled because they'd seen that tactic before. Each one of them, at one time or another, had been shocked by the Church Lady's earthy delivery and they enjoyed watching Evie's turn. It was an ear grabber that always worked. Today the gals were being treated to a show; admission, no charge.

The Church Lady pretended to regroup. She said, "… get yo' stuff together, so you can get on the right road. You need to wake up girl! The devil wanted whatever-it-was-that-brought-you-in-here to kill you, not to just send you on a steel-door vacation. You'd better recognize…'cause it was God who scooped you up outta suffocating waters, even though you didn't ask Him to."

"What?" Evie retorted. "You don't know that—where I been," she said. Her expression crinkled a bit because she didn't want to concede that the Church Lady seemed to know just where she'd been.

"God snatched you out of harm's way," the Church Lady said, "and put you inside of the whale's belly to pro-tect you until you could get your act together." The other inmates salted the Church Lady's speech with rousing Amens and ah-huhs. "You ever heard of Jonah? Never mind, I'll tell you about him later. But you need to know that it was God who told the devil to, 'Back-up off my child. Give her time to think.'"

Oh Lordy, Evie thought, *my mind's exhausted.*

"Now, Evie, don't you worry if you don't completely understand all that. I'll be here to help you, I promise. But in the meantime, I dare you to hold on." That's what Evie read in her secret Bible from Delta Dover. It resonated.

"If you don't give up on me. I won't give up on you," the Church Lady said compassionately with an endearing smile that Evie felt was just for her. "But all that is your choice. See that, girl? I bet you thought you didn't have any choices. Well, that's a lie from the pit of hell. You can always choose to survive. You'd better get into that Bible, girl. And check this out: sometimes—now, I know this happens with me all the time—just sometimes the stuff you end up in is a direct result of the choices only you have made—nobody else. And sometimes we tend to forget that."

"Ah, huhs" combed the air space once more. Some of the women raised their hands in praise and confirmation of having been there/done that. They eased themselves back in their desk chairs, grinned and rubbed their bellies as if they had just devoured a juicy steak.

The Church Lady stopped short in her little speech and switched gears, which left Evie hanging. "Hold up, girl," she said, holding up her right hand like it was a stop sign. She waved in the attention of the other women saying, "We're gonna do Bible study and we're gonna lift up your concerns and pray together, and all that stuff—just like always. Just let me give one little scripture to this young lady before we begin. Because she done got me all excited." The Church Lady cracked herself up and started laughing. Everyone else laughed too, everyone except Evie. She sat there stone faced.

"Evie," the Church Lady said, "so you're pissed off at God..."

I said I wasn't PISSSED! She screamed in her head.

"...and that's all right because He knows you're human and humans get pissed off from time-to-time. But don't worry, He's big and bad enough to handle it. And I am too."

Snickers and quiet Amens blanketed the room again. Evie, who still wasn't laughing, was too stunned and too needy to respond to anything. At least for now, though, the woman had her sincere attention.

The Church Lady continued, "some people say don't question God, but it's my opinion that if you've got a question, especially about yourself, who better to ask than God. Look in the New Testament, the book of James, near the back of the Bible." The Church Lady was always shelling out little directional cues like "near the back of the book" to help the women get used to locating the books in the Bible. She always gave them plenty of time. "It's James, chapter 1 and verses 5 through 8. It says that if you need wisdom you need to go ahead and ask. And that God won't correct you for asking. It also says that you must have faith in God, knowing He will answer you. Now, doesn't it make sense that God would answer you in time to help you...in time to stop more hurt from coming your way? [Again, she didn't give Evie time to answer] Evie, you asked me why He let this happen to you, why you are in here, well did you ask Him for any advice, prior to you coming in here?" The room fell silent. "Well, then, I think you've gotten your answer on that one. Now, it's time to move on to what's next for you, after you pay your back taxes on life. And I promise you that we'll work together on finding out what that is. But it's gonna depend on your growth of faith. Girl, I've got so much to say to you, I can hardly stand it. And we will get to it because you're worth it to me and to God. Just hold on, Evie, please, for me. Now, I know you just met me and I mean nothing to you at all, but I'm asking you to just hold on for me anyway," The Church Lady let out a laugh and said, "Hey, what you got to lose, if you do? 'Cause you already dead, right?" What she said was a sucker punch that tore open Evie's biggest secret.

"Now," the Church Lady spoke to everyone, "prayer concerns, anyone? What should we have on our hearts and minds as we go to the Lord in prayer?" The women, all except Evie, expressed prayer concerns for their children, husbands, boyfriends, upcoming court dates and anticipated release dates. Evie listened intently. They prayed for the other women in Cellblock K, who, like Evie, had refused to open up. Evie was astounded to discover that these women had been praying for her too. "Let's say a prayer," the Church Lady shouted and beckoned for them to stand, hold hands, and join her in an intimate huddle.

As the women around her lifted themselves out of their chairs, Evie, not sure of what to do, held back. Her body felt like warm pudding. If she got up, her body might spill all over the floor. Not wanting to be the center of attention again, she struggled to collect herself and join the others. The handholding part screamed, *this is too much*, but she extended her hands anyway.

Instinctively, the Church Lady kind of accidentally-on-purpose wandered over to Evie and cradled Evie's trembling hand inside her own. With heads bowed, eyes closed, the Church Lady broke the momentary silence with a soft chant of Hallelujahs. Evie felt the back of her eyes well up again and her lips quivered and creased. This time she didn't fight the feeling. She just let her tears go. They ended in the Lord's Prayer. Everyone, except Evie recited together.

After the prayer, the women returned to their seats. The Church Lady gave a light tug on Evie's hand, then peered directly into Evie's eyes before letting go. A connection forged. Evie felt her corpse loosening its grip on her soul. In almost a year, Evie had felt little more than hopelessness. Now, she felt her defenses breaking down. *What in the hell, I'ma going to do with this*? Evie thought, as she returned to her chair with her mind consumed in a haze of unclear thoughts.

"No more pain, no more hurt, no more stress…," the Church Lady recited the lyrics in rhythmic delight, "…when you let go of all the drama in your life, you can choose to win or lose. And I choose to win…"

"Mannn, those words sho' are powerful, huh," the Church Lady said. Evie held her Bible firm in her hand ready to pounce on the next set of scriptures the Church Lady would throw out. Maybe she would be the next one to read aloud. Maybe not. But the Church Lady changed gears.

"The title of this Bible study, ladies, is *No More Drama*," the Church Lady shouted. *That's it, No More Drama*, Evie alarmed within. She knew those words rang familiar.

The Church Lady continued, "I tell you, mannn, that Mary J. Blige sho-nuf hit it on the head when she sang that song," Laughter erupted in the room. Evie, astounded yet again, relaxed the cramped grip on her Bible and eased back in her chair. Mary was her favorite artist—her girl. She used to have every CD the artist put out! It was then, when Evie remembered that she could sing just like Mary could, maybe even better.

The Bible lesson moved on. The Church Lady quoted some scriptures and sandwiched them between the Mary J. Blige lyrics. Then, she seasoned them with her own personal life experiences. Evie sat there, chewing on everything said in the room.

Anyway, on that night, Day 77, the other women slowly got to know Evie and she got to know them. From that moment, they became her Bible Study classmates, not just inmates—or losers, as she liked to call them. These women were no longer monsters or natural enemies to Evie. *These are just some women with messed-up problems like mine*, she concluded in her mind, one day, lathering up in the shower. Now, on the flipside, they weren't bosom buddies, frolicking around at Disney World, either. Life was still pretty stinky. This was still jail and the future still looked bleak. But on this night, for Evie, something meaningful had begun to climb above the stench of her surroundings. Snippets of fresh air had seeped into Evie's lungs and she wanted to breathe again.

Evie never missed a Bible Study session after that and things got a little easier for her in the dayroom and rec room, too. Solitary mealtime was over. And sometimes it bordered on enjoyable. Her Bible-mates/her girls formed a protective hedge around her. If anybody wanted to start something, they had to get through them first. Every evening, alone in her cell, Evie thumbed through the pages of her secret Bible. It was uncanny how she always seemed to stop on a passage or written message that capped the day's events. What she read soothed emotional wounds, quenched new fears and applied to everything she heard. Evie was both confused and amazed by such revelation. Growing up, her momma kept a big black leather bound Bible poised on their cherry oak coffee table. Embroidered with fancy gold trim and thick gold lettering, it was the perfect centerpiece for the living room. It even had a name— Family Bible. They never opened it. It never occurred to Evie that they needed to open it or even if that was allowed. It was an ornament not a tool. Her mother always dusted it when she cleaned, or repositioned it just right. That was the most action it ever saw. They never took the Family Bible to church, when they went. Her mother had another, smaller Bible she used for toting around. That one stayed in the glove compartment of her car, so she wouldn't forget it.

In church, the pastor, the deacons, and all those old ladies dressed in white and sitting on the front pew acted like they had Bibles in their heads. If you needed to know something, you could just ask one of them. Throughout the service, they all shouted, waved their hands in the air and nodded their heads with great authority. It was impressive. Reading the Bible was for church folk, anyway, and old folk who had already lived their lives and didn't have anything else better to do. It wasn't for regular folk still dealing with real problems in a real world. And church folk didn't want you bothering them with anything real either. Evie found that out when she was a little girl.

One time, when Evie's mother lost one of her jobs and couldn't pay the rent, she went looking for some help down at the church they went to. She walked right up to the pastor, after church, and asked to speak to him. She did and he sent her to one of the deacons, who sent her to another deacon. Then that man pulled them all into a small huddle—her mother, Evie, and her sister, Roni—and told them to bow their heads. Little Evie kept her eyes open. She wanted to see God when He swooped down in the middle of their circle and solved everything. Pressed against the plush red carpet, the toes of eight black patent leather shoes framed the circle: two pointy-toed pumps, two sturdy wingtips, and four little Mary Janes, spit shined with Vaseline. Evie stared down into the void waiting for hope to arrive. When the man finished praying the circle broke up. Nothing happened. The smiling man sent them on their way, empty handed. Evie remembered the old deacon's last words to her teary-eyed mother. He said, "Don't worry, Sister. The Lord will provide." The Freemans moved shortly after that, evicted, and never went back to that church or any other church again.

chapter

FIVE

Day 117—almost four months in. It was a week after Thanksgiving and though she was used to having no visitors, somehow she thought that at least during the holidays, someone, her mother, her sister, or somebody would stop by, call, or write, or put some money into her account. What about Ray, couldn't he at least write from wherever he was? That night, in a dream, Evie was hard at work building a brick wall in the courtyard, planning to break out of jail. She piled heavy bricks, one on top of the other, but they mounted in an awful slant. It was supposed to look like the brick wall that Humpty Dumpty sat on, but it looked like a sliding board at the playground. Every time

Evie scaled the wall to the top, she slid back down again—back into her cell. Frustration forced her eyes open. She was breathless and surprised to be lying on her cot. Evie grabbed her secret Bible and flipped through the pages. Her fingers stopped in the Old Testament in the book of Amos, chapter 7. "I never heard of Amos," she whispered to herself. Verses 7- 8 were highlighted with a straight red line drawn around them and extended upward to a boxed-in note from Cookie.

> *From now on, you will be my plumb line. No more excuses. You've been harsh on me because I ignored the warning signs. But if you give me another chance at freedom, I promise I won't waste it. I Promise! Cookie M.*

Evie read the outlined scriptures that talked about a plumb line. They didn't soothe her. She was surprised and frightened. *How can God say He won't forgive you*, she thought. *I thought He was always supposed to forgive you*, she mused in her mind. She rushed backward, then forward throughout the Book of Amos, trying to find a happy ending. *Did Cookie get a second chance*, Evie wondered? *What about Anne, Delta and Rosalie?* Every day, their words spoke to her pain, confronted and comforted her. *But really*, Evie thought, lying there holding onto her Bible tightly, *what finally did happen to them?* And what was the book of Amos trying to tell her? Evie wanted to know.

The next evening was Bible Study. Eighteen women, in separate groups of six, shuffled into the classroom and filled every chair in the room. The Church Lady greeted them with her signature smile.

"Okay ladies," the Church Lady said authoritatively, "how many of you know that not everything in the Bible is touchy-feely. Really, almost none of it is. That's because surviving in this world is difficult. Living a quality life takes moving forward with a purpose. The Bible can teach you how to do that." The Church Lady swayed across the room and fanned her arms in slow motion to accentuate her next point. She said, "We live our lives, making foolish choices, taking stupid chances and expecting all the consequences to escape us." She stopped to stare at the group, intently staring right back at her. "Right up until the crap hits the fan," she declared, "or the crap dumps on our heads." Snickers abounded. She continued, "We're still thinking, 'how'd this happen to me?' And that's why we boldly ignore the warnings that God sends us." She paused to let her point soak in, then asked, "Y'all with me so far?" A resounding chorus of, "Amens," bellowed.

The Church Lady continued, "You know, ladies, prophets and messengers come in all shapes and sizes. But, often, when they come to warn us, we shun them, laugh at them, we may even cuss them. But we need to learn how to recognize godly warnings and take heed." Posted back in front of the huge wooden desk positioned in the front of the classroom, she reached for her glasses and her Bible and said, "Let's check out the Book of Amos in the Old Testament, chapter 7." Evie was dumbfounded. After a moment, the Church Lady added, "Whoever finds it first, please, shout out the page number. Thanks," she said, then moved on with her point, "The good news here…," the Church Lady said as the women thumbed through their Bibles, "is that we can learn from the hardheadedness of others. Let's read about an unlikely messenger named Amos and something called a Plumb Line." With one eyebrow raised she added, "A builder's tool for keeping things straight." Throughout the first half hour of the Bible study, the group hashed over the meaning of receiving bad news in time to do something about it. Revelation washed all over Evie.

During the next half hour, the Church Lady read from the Book of Esther, stressing a scripture that said, "…for such a time as this." Evie started feeling that maybe her incarceration was not an accident. Maybe it was her destiny, so that prophets could call out to her and this time she would be in a zone to listen. Later that night, Evie reexamined the Esther scripture in her secret Bible. Written in the margin was…

> *I was on my way to death and then I found you—here—in this awful place. It's funny, but I know now that I wouldn't have listened to you any place else. When I get out of here, I will help others see you as I do. I know I've been placed here for such a time as this. Esther 4: 14. Anne Sulley*

chapter

SIX

Day 148—almost five months in. It was New Year's Day and Evie had worked on her brain for three straight days, prior, to persuade herself that it was just another day on the calendar. It was nothing to get all crapped out about, just because she was starting the year behind bars. *This is a new beginning for me*, she churned repeatedly in her mind, *and it don't matter what the devil wants me to think. He's a goddamn…oops, sorry God…I mean, he's a liar—that's all… just a dirty liar!* A voice from the overhead interrupted her thoughts. "Library, ladies. If you're going, get in line—hurry up," a female C.O. announced from the control desk. Evie, sitting on her cot, scuffled to get the top half of her orange jumpsuit up and onto the upper part of her body. Hurriedly, she pushed her arms through the armholes and snapped up the front. Then she lunged for her beige sandals, scattered across the cell.

Inmates had an hour to peruse the shelves and the portable book carts for anything that caught their eye or they could just sit at the tables to study or write. They could buy composition books and pencils, rationed and accounted for. No more than seven inmates could be in the library at one time, Evie always liked to be amongst the first group. She was in there doing her usual browsing when she noticed something new on one of the book carts. It was a paperback, titled, *Raped At Birth* by Rosalie Mandy. *That name*, she thought. Her mind spun incredulous thoughts. *Could that be my Rosalie?* Her eyes fogged with moisture and curiosity. She stood there struggling for clarity. With a slow trembling hand, she reached out to pluck the book from its snug surroundings. As she cradled it in both hands, her teardrops dotted its front cover. Evie fanned the pages from front to back and breathed in the puff of air it created. For a moment, she just rested in the feel and the smell of it. Its worn pages smelled like nutmeg to her. When the moment passed she rushed to the back inside flap. She was hopeful for a description and maybe, even, a picture of the author. There it was. Evie inhaled one more breath. This time it was a breath of pleasure accompanied by an orgasmic sigh as she read the bio and inspected the photo before her. Rosalie's olive skin glowed. Her brown eyes sparkled with triumphant peace. Her features were full and contoured. She was beautiful. Her curly black hair hugged her face and complemented her huge toothy smile.

Rosalie Mandy's life was doomed before it began. She is the seed of a violent sexual attack—born of a white mother, and a black father, whom she would never know. Her family didn't want her. Friends took advantage of her love-starved vulnerability. Men abused her. Then she went to jail for something she didn't do. In jail, Mandy concluded that the only way out was suicide. However, a strange thing happened while she searched for death; she stumbled upon life. Mandy found God while incarcerated at the Charles County Correctional Facility in Maryland and He became her reason to live. Raped At Birth, is a riveting, touching, and inspirational story of survival. A must-read for anyone who is either lost in the valley or reaching out to someone imprisoned in the valley.

Mandy lives with her husband, Raphael, in White Plains, New York and their four children. She continues to write and share her awesome testimony at speaking engagements around the country.

Evie's fingers pulsated on the book; she held it so tight. When she found strength to move, she walked over to the volunteer librarian and checked the book out. Then she floated over to one of the tables, sat down and began reading. Evie could hardly believe it. Here was Rosalie, in the flesh. Well, almost in the flesh. Now she could find out all about her secret friend and confidant. By the time the library visit was over, Evie had almost a third of the two hundred-page book devoured. She would not leave her cell for the remainder of that day or night—not even for meals—until she finished reading. The book answered just about all of Evie's questions. She understood why Rosalie seemed so sad in some of her writings, perhaps the saddest of all her spiritual mentors—her angels. Rosalie's mother hated her and the small, predominately white town they lived in shunned and pitied her. "I grew up feeling like I had some kind of brand on my forehead," Rosalie wrote on page fifty. She left the Maryland suburb and moved to Washington, D.C., where things got worse instead of better. On the fateful night before her arrest, she and a couple of her girlfriends were riding around, club hopping. They were drinking and smoking weed, and driving under the influence, Rosalie admitted in her book. Evie read so fast, she had to slow herself down several times, so her mind could catch up with her eyes. She yearned for a full mental soak in the meaning of every word. Rosalie's girlfriend, Jesa, was behind the wheel and killed some young boy on his way to work at Seven-Eleven. Frightened, she skidded away from the scene of the accident and out of Rosalie's life.

> *We were all pretty wasted*, Rosalie wrote, *but the screeching of brakes, the loud thump, and the feel of rolling over something, perhaps a bicycle, a log, or a body,*
> *I don't know which, sobered us up quick-fast. Jesa mashed down on the gas with her foot and all of our heads jerked backward as the car—my car—coughed, spat and burnt rubber, then, we sped off in a cloud of road dust and debris. When we got to our neighborhood, we all made a vow never to tell anyone what happened. It was a vow un-kept because the police knocked on my door the next morning.*

Rosalie's words dripped off the page like melted butter. In jail, Rosalie was put on a suicide watch, she was so depressed. During those first few weeks, she didn't remember much more than her non-stop crying, she wrote in her book, except for the one thing she swore she'd never forget. It was how the Chaplain walked in her cell to see her and handed her a Bible before he left. Rosalie remembered how she first thought it strange that he would give her a worn-out, used Bible. It had markings and highlights written in it by some women named Anne Sulley and Cookie Mendoza. Rosalie wrote how she only started reading the notes because she was bored and had nothing else to do, nothing else to lose. Before long, Rosalie explained, the words mutated into meaning and cleared a pathway to God. Evie was floored to find out that Rosalie's time in that same jail was back in the late '80s. Her release date was November 3, 1990.

chapter

SEVEN

Day 200—six months in. It was Ray's birthday. Evie woke up thinking about it. Though she had managed to loosen Ray's daily grip around her heart, the way he was yanked out of her life caused her to think about him more than she wanted. She wondered just how long would he hang on her mind.

She was alone, that day, in the rec. room because most of her girls, in her Bible study crew, had gone to a new drug treatment program the jail offered. Evie stretched out on a mat kind of faking at doing some push-ups when a new woman appeared out of nowhere and threw her mat down on the floor beside her. Evie made the quick observation of how, since this was jail, and that you clearly had to be a female, housed with other females—that this particular female looked male—close-cropped haircut and all. It wasn't a shocker; just an occasional occurrence. The woman slowly rested her body down on her mat, and Evie felt uncomfortable. She tried to blow off the weirdness by flipping over and switching to body crunches. Careful of the C.O.'s watchful eye, the woman brushed her hand over Evie's breasts then brandished a Cat-in-the-hat grin. Next, she let her hand drop over and downward on the inside of Evie's thigh. Evie reflexed upward onto her feet and stared disgustedly at the woman. Delighted by it all, the woman sat up, checked out the C.O., who now wasn't paying attention, and whispered to Evie, "Don't act like you don't like it. Just wait 'til later, Boo." Evie stood there momentarily frozen by surprise and fright. *What-the-f...?* She thought. Finally, she just turned, grabbed her mat and walked over to the other side of the room.

Over the months, Evie had seen plenty of weird sexual stuff go down in that place. Sometimes it seemed like some inmates didn't care what they did or who saw them doing it. But, until that day, none of that crap had managed to brush up against her leg. Fifteen minutes floated by and her thigh still tingled from the unwanted touch.

There were moments, in the stillness of the night, when Evie felt claustrophobic. When she gave in to it, she felt like she was smothering in an airtight cage of anguish. This night (after the rec. room incident) was one of those nights. Lying on her cot, Evie tried hard to hear one of the Church Lady's endurance talks. "Close your eyes and see yourself in another place," Evie chanted to herself in a whisper, like the Church Lady had instructed her to do. She whispered one more, "I'm too good for this. I know there's something better for me. I will get to it, if I just hold on." That night, Evie's mind and flesh wrestled until dawn. She pressed to envision the brighter future that the Church Lady forecasted, but no visions manifested. After a while, her thoughts mused into murky visions of Ray.

Gently, his arms wrapped around her body. He squeezed tight and began perspiring on her stomach and between her thighs, and beneath the fold of her breasts. His kisses caused pearls of sweat to dampen her hairline. He kissed harder and the pearls exploded and trickled down her forehead. Evie struggled to push his memory up off her, but it wasn't doing any good. "I'm better than this," she cried softly, "You left me. You don't deserve me. I deserve better than you and I'm gonna get it too," she protested, but her voice was only a helpless whimper, as she struggled to overcome his intenseness. Her resistance was cloaked in darkness from head to toe under the covers. Ray inched underneath and conquered the entire lower half of her body. Evie's muscles locked in a spasm of emotion. Her pelvis and thighs seized up in place. Guilty pleasure rushed in like a strong ocean wave. She could do nothing, but welcome it. When the tide rolled out, it left her drenched in sweat and panting under her blanket. In seconds, another pleasure wave rushed in. The afterglow drenched her in shame and disappointment. Defeated, Evie mopped her forehead with the back of her hand and whispered to herself, "What a damn shame, raped by a freakin' memory." She'd suffered a setback and she knew it.

Lying on her cot in the predawn, Evie retrieved her Bible from its hiding place and allowed her trembling moist fingers to race to the book of Hebrews. To find it, she had to position her opened Bible in just the right angle to catch the beam of courtyard light, funneled through her cell window. She found herself reading chapter 13, verses 5 and 6. She read that one part, repeatedly, "I will never leave you nor forsake you." The Church Lady told her that that didn't mean she'd never have a setback or that she would never be knocked down. It meant that no matter what happened, God would always be there to get her through it. "Setbacks are fertile ground for comebacks," she remembered the Church Lady saying. Then she read some stuff before the verses and some stuff after them, just as one of her older jail-mates advised her to do. Desperation had pushed her to read those words on other occasions and that night desperation had forced her to read them again. Evie had just about memorized those verses. She'd also memorized Rosalie's words written right beside them.

> *The Lord helps me! Why should I be afraid of what people can do to me? Real or imagined. (also read Matthew 21:18-22. That's good too!) Rosalie Mandy*

Here was one of Rosalie's notes where she didn't sound so sad, Evie noticed. In fact, she sounded encouraged. Perhaps Rosalie wrote it near the time of her release, Evie reasoned. Evie's fingers hurried to the book of Matthew, chapter 21. It was another one of her favorites because in her mind, Ray was the fig tree, all withered up because he produced nothing good in her life. Jail was the mountain, mentioned in the scripture, that she had to cast into the sea. A fresh start, that's what she'd ask Jesus for, once she figured out what that meant. Searching and finding Rosalie's thoughts was like being on an exploration in the desert. It was like stumbling upon water. She found herself searching for and climbing wonderful pyramids of wisdom on the journey. Suddenly she wasn't in her cell at all, her mind and spirit had been transported out and was free to go wherever she pleased them to go. Morning came early in jail. Feeling a little better, she slammed her Bible shut, put it back in its place and tried to grab some more shut-eye before lights-on ushered in the intrusive stomp of C.O. combat boots.

That evening, the Church Lady stood by the class-room door and smiled that same huge smile like she always did, the one expected to bring world peace and cure cancer. She greeted the women as they sauntered in, happy to see her, and sat down. There were always a few newcomers sprinkled in the group, so the Church Lady always took a few moments to introduce herself. Right away, Evie honed in on the Church Lady's added excitement like it was Christmas or something. The group had hardly prayed inside their usual huddle and settled back into their seats before she started talking.

"You gotta get tight with Jesus," the Church Lady said like it just came to her. "I mean, you want him to be your boy. Yo dawg! Your own personal NWA; your own personal nigga-with-an-attitude. You know what I mean?" Now the Church Lady was always working hard at trying to be hip and current with today's lingo. And the women gave her points for that. Still it was also funny to see her work so hard at it. But she had a knack for taking religious tradition out of their worship. It was clear to them that what she shared wasn't for show, it was for real. And they liked it whenever she put Jesus in the 'hood—their 'hood. "God is a lifesaver," she often said, "not a pew warmer. He wants to be in your heart more than he wants your butt on some church pew." She added with a laugh, "But don't forget church all together, now. 'Cause we need it."

"You want Him in your posse. To do that, you've got to study Him, inside and out, acknowledge that He knows you, loves you, and has a glorious plan for you! Girrrl, if you don't believe me, just look at the book of Jeremiah, 29:11-14. It's all right there and more." The sound of pages fluttering in the air and voices calling out the page number of the scripture was music to the Church Lady's ear. It was the sound of success. The women competed with each other to be the first to read aloud. Evie was the winner. She knew the scripture because Cookie had outlined it in red ink and had drawn lines to her penned inner thoughts.

Strive to thrive in spite of your present surroundings.
The words straddled the topside margin and connected to more notes, written in the bottom side margin.
God will make prophets out of prisoners.
Another line arrowed downward to something written on the bottom margin.
This was a promise, but the people had to keep their end of it for it to come true."
Cookie Mendoza

"You've been set aside to rediscover the dream in your belly," the Church Lady stressed like her life depended on it. Her voice got louder, as it often tended to do, when she said, "Discovered without the interference of those up-close-and-personal unbelievers you been hangin' with. You know what I mean: that no-good-man…two-faced friend…jealous relative and so on. Read Exodus 32: 25-29. Moses gives the people a command from the Lord. All those who stood for the Lord were ordered to kill all those who did not—even if that meant killing friends and relatives. And for all those who obeyed, God acknowledged that such a thing was hard to do, and He blessed them." Then, the Church Lady cautioned, "Now don't go out here and commit murder or nothing," she laughed, kind of, "But you can erase all those people you know don't mean you any good, from your life. And you can start doing that right now. Evie…," she said.

Why did she single me out, Evie thought, but she felt honored.

"…I promise you, when it's time for someone in the flesh to see the new you, they will—and they'll see the new you without you having to prove a thing or utter a word," the Church Lady declared. A flood of Amens gushed throughout the room. Tears skipped down Evie's cheeks. Hope embroidered her heart.

"I've got a video to show you," the Church Lady announced. The women immediately began shuffling chairs, securing prime viewing spots in front of the huge television mounted on a portable cart. "I know some of you are already fans of this evangelist," she said as she turned to allow the VCR to swallow the tape. Evie was clueless.

The blue screen flickered into gray snow, then refreshed into music and a collage of colored picture stills. An announcer moved into view and introduced the speaker, "Stay tuned for Evangelist Anne Sulley with another moving message from God!" Evie was sitting in her chair with her legs folded under the desk. At the mention of Anne's name, she couldn't believe her ears. A tall, slender woman graced center stage. Her complexion was a peachy orchid, radiating light. Throughout her sermon, she slowly sauntered back and forth across the stage, and addressed the arena-sized audience. Anne's black hair had strands of blended auburn, was cut in a neat bob and tapered at the back of her neck. Her ears and wrists were outfitted in fine jewelry and her slender body was garbed in a stylish light blue pantsuit. The hem of her pleaded pant legs danced off the heels of her glass slippers. Evie, void of all life forms except her own, sat attentive, motionless, and speechless.

That's my Anne, all right, Evie surmised. She was surprised to discover that Anne was a white woman and that she was an older woman, maybe in her fifties or sixties, even. Anne's testimony was riveting. The women cheered when she mentioned being incarcerated at the Charles County Correctional Facility back in the early '80s. Her release date was January 28, 1983. Anne found God in jail and, in doing so, she said, she discovered that she had a gift to preach. She even began her formal theology training while still in jail. After her release, she'd even reconciled with her adoptive parents.

"Today," Anne said, "my traveling ministry is worldwide and that's nothing but the grace of God." The crowd roared. She continued, "Not bad for a dropout and a jailbird, huh." The testimony went further. Anne mentioned that her first time reading a Bible was in jail. Anne said, "I began studying scriptures and jotting notes down on the front flap of my Bible so I wouldn't forget what I learned or how I felt at that moment. I'd write notes, right there on the pages." She laughed and pointed at the Bible she held. "Besides," she added, "whoever had the Bible before me had done the same thing. I loved that little Bible! It became my security blanket. I wanted to take it with me when I got out of jail, but somehow I lost it. But that didn't stop me from reading God's word," she shouted, "I got a new Bible!" The audience roared. "I just continued on with my next Bible," she said, "and the next one after that." Anne held up her Bible again, showing off the front flap. A camera zoomed in to reveal written markings inside. "A clean, undisturbed Bible is no testimony at all," she shouted. Evie's mind raced back to her mother's Bible that sat untouched on their living room coffee table.

Anne preached on above the noise that resonated approval, "If God can bless me—an angry, defeated lonely woman—'cause that's who I was when I went to jail—then He can bless you if you let Him." That was her last word before the Church Lady hit the stop button on the VCR. The flash of the blue screen jolted Evie back into the reality of her surroundings. She looked around and there was not a dry eye in the room. "Let's pray," the Church Lady called out, knowing that nothing else needed to be said. Evie was convinced she had just seen a miracle and an angel—again.

chapter

EIGHT

DAY 275—nine months in. Evie was feeling invincible. *Half my time is done and I'm still standing*, she boasted inside. She'd completed her GED program her first time out. Some of the inmates had to go through it several times. She was getting much revelation from God, through her Bible studies and her private reading. She started scribbling down her own spiritual observations in her secret Bible, just like her mentors had done.

"Now I know that you will give me beauty for my ashes. Flowers for my sorrow and joy to heal my

broken heart. Is. 61: 1-4. I just have to hold on.
Evie Freeman"

She wrote her note in the side margin next to the scripture.

Yes, it was still terrible that she was in jail, but now she was convinced her experience had a point. Evie never missed a Bible Study session or a Sunday church service, led by rotating strands of faith. Sometimes it was Catholic, sometimes Baptist, sometimes African Methodist Episcopal (A.M.E.), sometime Lutheran, sometimes it was nondenominational. She even felt comfortable sharing her singing talents and reveled in the approval it brought her from inmates and the Christian volunteers. She couldn't remember receiving approval like that, ever. Evie and a couple of the other women formed a choir for the church services. Listening to her soft, sultry voice was like being cradled on a cloud, enjoying a warm gentle breeze.

Evie had the jail routine mastered. She still hadn't heard from anybody on the outside, but so what. Her family was inside, now, and they supported her. This was jail, however, so there were always the little extras, as she called them. Negative personalities sprung up without notice. The hardcore troublemakers usually kept to themselves, choosing to make trouble with each other, which was good because it kept them alternating their time in an isolation cell—ISO is what the C.O.s called it. They didn't usually bother the church-folk crew out of some kind of weird, laughable respect. It was as if, they felt that just in case there was a God, maybe they'd get some brownie points for not kicking the church-folk behinds. However, they fought and cursed each other on the regular. The church-folk crew traveled in packs, anyway. Hassling one of them was just too much trouble. Besides the church-folk crew and the troublemakers, there were the cracked-out druggies. They just sat around in corners, nodding in and out of awareness on jail-issued drugs, intended to wean them off the street stuff, and to keep them manageable in the lockup.

In the middle of the night, Evie was startled awake by the glare of a C.O.'s flashlight. "Sorry Freeman, you got incoming," the C.O. said. "Meet your new friend, Trent—Tina Trent," said a second C.O., as she muscled the woman into the cell and shoved her down on the other cot. Evie knew that the C.O.'s rough treatment was unusual, but was too groggy to make sense of it. The shove caused Trent to drop her linen and blankets on the floor. "Get in there, Trent. I don't feel like no more mess outta you," the first C.O. said as he clanged the cell door shut. Evie listened to their footsteps fade as they walked down the hall.

Instinctively, Evie sat up and attempted to help the woman pick up her linen. "Get the hell away from me," the woman snapped, "I got it. Just get the hell back over there where you come from." For an instant, a narrow band of courtyard light streaming in the window illuminated the woman's sandy brown face. The most vile, surly, wild expression, from eyebrows to chin, materialized. Evie's mouth gaped open and she gasped as if she'd seen a monster.

Tina snarled, "What the hell you lookin' at?"

"Nothin'," Evie said in a bold sarcastic tone. She collected her wits in a hurry because this wasn't the time to show fear. Evie reclined back down on her cot, feigning unconcern. She cautiously pulled the cover up around her shoulders, but didn't face the wall, like usual. She didn't dare turn her back.

As dawn crept in, Evie awoke to find the woman, sitting on the edge of her still unmade cot, staring at her. "I can't sleep," Tina said and without warning started snatching Evie's blanket right off her body. Evie jerked the blanket back as a reflex action. Drowsy, she hardly recalled the woman entering the cell at all.

"You better let go," Tina demanded, "or you gonna get your ass kicked."

"You crazy, dog-face heifer! Get the hell away from me! Who are you, anyway?"

"Let go, Bitch!" Tina said.

"Hell no!" The two women toppled off the edge of Evie's cot and scuffled onto the floor.

"You gonna gimme that shit you wearin', too," Tina gritted. The woman had twenty pounds on Evie and with a violent jerk, she ripped the blanket out of Evie's hands with one final pull. Tina pounced her musty body on top of Evie and pinned her to the floor using her knees. The wafting stench clogged Evie's nostrils and her eyes watered. Tina tore wildly at Evie's top and undershirt, and slapped Evie's bare chest, blue and purple. Evie screamed when Tina punched her in the face. She squirmed and struggled to break free. Finally, with a gush of angry strength, she twisted her wiry torso back and forth to rock the madwoman off balance. As Tina toppled over like Goliath, Evie managed to kick Tina as hard as she could in the back with her foot.

"Oh, now, you gonna get what you askin' for," Tina threatened, struggling to get up and regain her power. She growled like a pit bull with rabies. Spit balls sprayed from her mouth when she spoke and her breath smelled like a stopped-up toilet.

"Stay offa me," Evie screamed.

"Strip, Bitch!"

The shouting and tussling, finally summoned the C.O.s. They rushed in and pulled the two women apart, who were by this time, tussling on the floor grabbing wads of each other's hair.

"Get that heifer outta here," Evie yelled, breathless and bleeding from both eyes. Totally exposed, she scrambled to cover her chest with the remnants of her bloody undershirt, ripped off her body. "That wild dog tried to kill me for no reason."

Two male C.O.s dragged Tina out of the cell, kicking and screaming obscenities clear down the hall.

The sun made its full appearance, but Evie couldn't see it because her eyes were nearly swollen shut. Every inmate on Cellblock K awakened a tad bit earlier, that day, because of the commotion. Some spied Evie holding a white, blood-splattered towel against her face on her way to sick call. Every bone in her body cried out in pain. She sat down gingerly on a bench positioned outside of the doctor's office, trying to piece together what had happened and why. *Especially when things were going so good*, she thought.

A female C.O. sat with Evie until the doctor called her inside. "You'll be all right Evie. Hold on," she whispered.

Hold on to what, Evie thought.

Evie had never been to sick call though she saw others go plenty of times. "Come on in, young lady," said a cheery voice from inside the office. The C.O. helped Evie to her feet and led her into the office, then disappeared. There the doctor stood, an attractive black woman with a smooth Hershey chocolate complexion. Her long black dreads were pulled back into a ponytail. Some of the braids were darted with tiny beige and brown seashells. The doctor was medium height, shapely and outfitted in an unbuttoned starched white doctor's jacket, draped over a lima bean green shirtdress. By this time, one of Evie's eyes had swollen completely shut and the other eye brandished a bluish-reddish/greenish crescent around its rim.

"Oooh, girrrl, you look like a Christmas tree," the doctor said, then chuckled, trying to lighten the mood. Evie noticed a slight Caribbean curl to her tone.

"What in the world happened to you?" The doctor said in a lighthearted voice, but the mood-lightening wasn't taking effect.

"I got attacked for no reason by some crazy animal."

"Well, that animal sho' was crazy and it hits hard, huh."

The joking still wasn't funny and it got on Evie's nerves. Her eyes throbbed.

"Yeah!" Evie said.

"Did she bite you anywhere?"

"No, I don't think so."

"Did you bite her anywhere?"

"Hell no!"

"Okay, girrrl, settle down. I always have to ask, you know," the doctor said slowly while examining Evie's facial and chest wounds. She gave Evie two tiny pills for the pain, plus an injection cocktail to ward off infection or worse.

"There now, nothing's broken. I don't think anything's permanently damaged. You'll be good-as-new in a week or two."

"If you say so," Evie's voice trembled. She wanted to cry, but couldn't.

"Well, I say so," the doctor retorted with a smile. "I'll take another look at you next Tuesday. It was a good thing this happened today," she laughed. Evie strained to give her an evil glare.

"I'm only here on Tuesday's and Thursdays. But they would have sent you to the hospital emergency room."

"Yeah, I'm real lucky," Evie said, sarcastically.

This was a real blow to her metamorphosis into Christianity. She hadn't been mad at God in months, but today she was plenty pissed at Him. Moreover, she was confused. *Why did God let this happen*, she thought, *what did I do wrong?*

"Well, Miss Evie Freeman," the doctor said, looking at Evie's wristband to confirm the name. "I gave you some pain medication and I'll leave instructions for the nurse to continue the meds, every four hours, as needed. You let someone know if you continue to feel great discomfort. Okay? My name is Dr. Dover and I'll be back on Thurs…"

DOVER!! Evie exploded in her brain, *this can't be happening!* The rest of what the doctor said trailed off into the abyss because Evie, stunned by the name, could no longer hear her. Until that time, she hadn't really given the doctor direct eye contact, she couldn't. But now, with her diminishing-good eye, she struggled to focus. Evie zeroed in on the woman's nametag, pinned to her white jacket. She read it: *Dr. Delta Dover.* Evie gulped. Her throat was sore.

She tried desperately to scan the office for any name-identifying diplomas. The framed diploma and the nametag on the desk confirmed it.

"Doctor, doctor yyyour name," Evie stuttered, "sssounds familiar...I..."

"Ahhh, yes, baby girl," Delta responded with a laugh and a warm smile. She walked over to Evie and carefully patted her bruised back with the assurance of a consoling mother, "I imagined someone here has told you about me, huh. How long have you been in here, child?"

"About nine months," she responded quickly, "But, no, no one told me anything. I think I saw your name on something...I think I saw it in my..."

"Well, Evie," the doctor cut her off, "a long time ago I was exactly where you are today—in jail [her voice tone dipped]—right here," She chuckled with recollection, while she milled about the office, returning things to their shelves as she talked, "but I got myself together and you can too."

"But I believe I saw your na..." Evie's mouth was open and lodged in the middle of her word when she was clipped by a glimpse of the C.O.'s uniform. Evie's jaws snapped shut like a crocodile capturing escaping prey. The C.O. escorted a stunned Evie back to her cell. It was all cleaned up and a single again. On the way down the hall, Evie turned and looked at the C.O. and attempted to ask a question.

"Do you know if..."

"Turn around, Freeman," she said sternly, "No talking in the hallway. You know that." Evie pointed her head forward and continued the walk in silence. She did not have a long-term roommate for the rest of her sentence, especially not one coming down off a PCP high.

During the next library run, Evie asked the Chaplain if he knew about Dr. Dover. Did he know that she had been in jail; an inmate, right there, even? He smiled and gave her a Xeroxed copy of a newspaper article that he seemed, Evie noticed, to have at-the-ready. It was dated December 29, 2003. Evie sat down to inspect it thoroughly.

> Delta Dover, a former inmate in the Charles County Correctional Facility, was released on December 23, 1997. Back in 1996, Dover was a med student on her way to becoming a doctor when she had a run-in with the law. While on a semester break, she was nabbed at an airport with a package of marijuana sewn into the lining of her coat. But that was then and this is now. Today Dover is heading back to jail for loftier reasons— and she says that she can't wait to get there.

"Dover found God in jail," the story revealed, "and that's what turned this would-be trafficker back on her intended course of becoming a physician. 'I found strength in this little Bible they gave me,' said Dover, 'It had all these inspirational thoughts in it, written by other inmates who had the Bible before me. Their thoughts became my inspiration not to give up while I was in jail. That little Bible kept me sane. It was my lifeline.'"

The article went on about Dr. Dover's life and survival in jail. It told of how her distraught parents kept fighting for her release and how their reputation in the community, together with Delta's good behavior and remorseful attitude finally afforded her a second chance to pursue her career.

A photo of a younger cap-and-gown Delta accepting her medical degree from Duke University graced the top of the page.

It was her all right, Evie thought.

Then the article talked about how she'd planned to return home to dedicate her medical career to the health and well-being of underprivileged women and to those incarcerated searching for fresh chances. "My experience turned my life around," Delta said in the article.

When Evie reached the story's end, she leaned back in her chair and let tears of joy salt her cheeks. "You can keep that," the Chaplain walked by and said.

"Thanks," Evie responded, weak and grateful. She neatly folded the article with plans to tuck it inside her Bible as soon as she could return to her cell. The next week, with both eyes open and in natural color, Evie had a second appointment with the Doctor. On a third visit, she decided to go out on a limb and engage Delta in an intimate talk, divulging that she was now in possession of the Bible. A friendship bloomed. Evie finally had a regular visitor coming to the jail to see her. During one of those visits, Delta said, "I'll be here for you when you get out of here. I'm not joking." There was a relief pause. The doctor said, "I know what it's like."

A barely audible, "Thank you," graced with a shaky smile was all that Evie could muster.

chapter

NINE

Day 365—one year in. Evie felt that she was on the downside of her wilderness journey. Still, six months was nothing to sneeze at, but now there was light at the end of the tunnel. Evie graduated from the in-house laundry job to work-release. She worked the day shift at the nearby McDonald's. Hauling big, heavy crates of lettuce all day made her vow never to eat a salad again in life. "Okay, I know that's wrong," she joked to herself, one afternoon in the middle of her hauling. Evie walked back and forth to work, except for the days when the doctor was around to give her a lift. The ride gave them more opportunity to talk.

Evie's experiences with the Church Lady were great and rich with revelation. She brought in more sermons from Anne Sulley and happened to bring in readings from Rosalie's second book, titled, *Life, the Second Time Around.* Evie thought it was even more inspirational than the first book, though nothing could top the feeling she had when she discovered it.

"Hey, Evie how's it going," Delta said, during one of their visits. They sat in one of those little compartment booths with a table and glass partition separating them. But that wasn't no big thing, they both knew the deal and they dealt with it. During their frequent visits, Evie shared her dreams and aspirations with the doctor. Evie learned that the doctor had a lucrative practice in Georgetown, but ran a free health clinic on wheels in poor neighborhoods every third Saturday; that was in addition to volunteering at the jail. Evie now fathomed dreams of a singing career and she shared her dreams with Delta Dover. It was an aspiration, buried beneath her pain for so long she had forgotten about it until the Church Lady's nagging questions helped dig it up. Now, she even threw around the notion of maybe using her singing as a form of ministry. Possibilities were sprouting in her mind.

"Hey Doctor D. Thanks for coming."

Delta smiled. "Well, it's your anniversary, girl. I wouldn't have missed it for the world. What-up today?" Delta laughed.

"Nothin'. I'm just holdin' on. Thankin' God for lastin'," Evie said with a sigh. "You know? I'm up 365 days and I'm still alive."

"Good. Stay that way. We've got things to do," the doctor said, then abruptly added, "Hey Evie…"

"What?"

"You still got that Bible?"

"You know I do. Why?"

"Well, I've been talking to Cookie and she…"

"COOKIE!"

"Yeah, Cookie. Cookie Mendoza. You said you still had the Bible, right?"

"Of course I do. You know I do," Evie said in a shouting whisper. "You mean to tell me you know Cookie Mendoza, that's in my Bible?"

"Yeah," Delta said. She was low key on purpose, teasing Evie.

"You never told me that. How come you never told me THAT?"

"You never asked." Delta smirked and smiled mischievously. She couldn't help it. It was funny.

Knowing Cookie was a big juicy steak that Delta had to hold back for just the right moment. She had to be sure of where Evie's head was at before she served it up.

"I know Anne and Rosalie too!" She let on.

Evie wanted to faint, but she knew the chain to which she was handcuffed wouldn't let her drop. So all she could do was remain frozen and speechless. Her tongue grew heavy and her mouth flung open.

"Close your mouth, little girl, before the flies buzz in." Delta joked. Evie obeyed, but the blank stare remained. "Anyway, I've been talking to Cookie. I told her about you and she thinks she can help you. You know, with your singing and all that."

"When was she in here? Evie asked, "When did she get out? Where is she now? What did she do to get herself locked up?"

Mendoza, found guilty for embezzlement, received a fifteen-year sentence in a Federal prison. During her brief stint at the Charles County Correctional Facility, before extradition, her bosses rallied on her behalf. She was of exceptional character, they said, a person under tremendous pressure. They also strongly reminded the judge how she was returning the money when nabbed. Miraculously, Mendoza served only two years with eight years' probation. Slowly, due to the grace of some former colleagues, Mendoza rebuilt her life and climbed to the top. During a television interview that was later reported on in *Life Magazine*, Mendoza said that, "God made me the poster child for comebacks and I am both humbled and proud of my new role." But Evie would hear Cookie's testimony straight from Cookie—later—Delta felt. Now was not the time.

"Woaw, woaw, slow down girl," Delta said, "You can ask her all that when you meet her." Evie gulped, again, and her eyes bucked. She continued, "But, I think Cookie was in here somewhere, back in the '70s. Even before Anne. Cookie Mendoza is Inez Mendoza." There was a pregnant pause. Evie wasn't familiar with the name. "You know, chairwoman of the Equal Employment Opportunity Commission, appointed by the President of the United States.

Evie hardly believed her ears. She didn't quite know what all that *Equal Commission* stuff was, but she understood the significance of the *President of the United States* part. She knew that was big.

"Evie, girl, Cookie's got all kinds of connections—everywhere. For that matter, so do Anne and Rosalie. If you play your cards right, girl—honey—you're about to blow up and I mean in a good way." There was a couple of seconds of dead air again. Evie was feeling lightheaded and couldn't speak.

"I've heard what you've got in those pipes of yours and those songs you wrote were off the hook."

There was silence. Delta stared at Evie, waiting for her reaction.

"What's the matter, girl. Cat got your tongue?" Delta said, thoroughly pleased with herself. She threw her head back roaring in laughter.

Evie wanted to say, yeah, or something, but evidently, the cat did have her tongue, so all she could do was cry.

Delta laughed some more. "Don't cry, girl! You know that tightens up the pipes. Sing! Sing!"

"I don't know what to…I mean, I never dreamed…," Evie responded in a weak and shaky voice, "…God is so good. I don't know what else to say. Thank you, Doc. Thank y…"

"Nothing else to say, girl, you're right, God Is Good," Delta said, forgetting that she couldn't hand her the tissue she had just fished out of her pocket, so she wiped her own nose with it.

"Evie, can you hear me, girl; you paying attention?"

"Yes," she said, weakly, then nodded to confirm.

"Keep your head up. In a while, you ain't gonna have nothin' but joy." Delta added discreetly, "Keep this to yourself, you hear me? And keep praying. Your time's coming, sooner than you think."

Their time was up. They stood up and let their eyes say goodbye, while the C.O. stood waiting to take Evie back to the cellblock. Before she disappeared through the door, she turned to take one more look at the doctor, kind of checking to see if she was real. Delta hadn't taken her eyes off Evie. She mouthed a quick, "Seeya later."

Delta didn't tell Evie during that visit, but she and Cookie were also working on an early release for Evie. She didn't want to say anything in case things fell through, but things looked good. Evie had nothing but good behavior served in jail. She had just about paid off her restitution be-cause she kept almost no money for herself and a positive work release record earned her days off her sentence. Evie hadn't even realized how much all that was operating in her favor.

The months marched on. Evie kept praying, kept sing-ing with her church-folk crew, kept hauling crates of lettuce, kept her nose clean—and Delta kept her promise.

Day 399—marked thirteen months and a very good day. The brisk Wednesday afternoon glided into a cool evening without fanfare. It was 5:29 p.m. on September 8, 2004. A burnt-orange sunset washed over the granite facil-ity. The surrounding silver barbed wire fence shimmered in the descending light. Its pointy edges sparkled like stars. Evie Freeman emerged. She was dressed in a borrowed pair of jeans, sneakers and a sweatshirt, courtesy of Delta, and she focused on the front lobby as she moved forward accompanied by her last C.O. escort.

Anne, Rosalie, Delta and Cookie sat in a spit-shined black-on-black, four-door, 2005 CLS Mercedes coupe, awaiting Evie's emergence from the facility's double doors.

Cookie was behind the wheel and popped open the trunk, so Evie could throw in her scant belongings. They were packaged in a worn, bulky 8 x 10 manila envelope. Evie smiled at the rolled-up tinted window. The back door swung open and she was swallowed inside. The women had a lot to do that evening and a lot to discuss. Their dinner reservation at *B. Smith's* in D.C. was at 7:30 p.m. and it was imperative that they make a quick stop at the St. Charles Mall, first.

Evie left her secret Bible where she found it, under the same corner between her mattress and cot spring. She had plans to start over with a new one.

###

The Prison Plumb Line
—a novella

Discussion Questions:

1. How did Evie's special Bible get into her cell?
   Who do you think put it there and why?

2. What was Evie's major setback while in jail?
   Have you ever experienced a major setback in your Christian walk?
   If so, what was your *reaction*?
   Are you still holding on for the *victory*?
   Is there a *comeback* story?

3. Why was everyone in Evie's inner circle thrust out of her life?
   Do you think that was by God's design? Why or why not?

4. Like Evie, have you ever encountered angels in unlikely places or times in your life?
   How did you know? Discuss.

5. Second chances to change: does Evie deserve a second chance?
   Why or why not?

About the Author

Yvonne J. Medley is a features writer and photographer, who has worked on staff at *The Washington Times* and has reported for several publications, such as *The Washington Post, People Magazine, Gospel Today Magazine, A Time to Love Magazine* and other national and local publications. Medley garnered recognition for controversial pieces on racism and the church, and the psychology of sexually abusive clergy.

Medley travels the country, interviewing and writing about intriguing personalities as well as *everyday* heroes, proving that everyone has a riveting and beneficial story to tell. One only needs to make a quality effort to unearth it.

She conducts her *Life Journeys Writing Workshops (LJWW),* designed to empower and encourage. Some of these workshops have been supported by the Maryland Humanities Council's *One Maryland: One Book* program.

She's conducted LJWWs for The Maryland Writers' Association's *22nd Annual Writers' Conference,* the State of Maryland's *Big Read* program, The Reginald F. Lewis Museum of African American History & Culture, as well as various area educational programs and churches.

Medley is the founder of *The Life Journeys Writers Club,* serving writers in Southern Maryland and beyond. She also teaches ESL (English as a Second Language) and ABE (Adult Basic Education) adult learners. Medley is a *Point of Change Jail & Street Ministry, Inc.* volunteer, dedicated to uplift and impact the lives of incarcerated men and women, their families, and provide aftercare support and life skills training.

Medley is a wife and mother of four, and lives in Waldorf, Maryland. For events and book signings, connect with Medley at www.yvonnejmedley.com or send an email to info@yvonnejmedley.com .

❖   ❖   ❖

Made in the USA
Charleston, SC
26 September 2013